A LITTLE

A DOGS GUIDE to
DRAGONS

← by Wolfie

Leo Hartas
&
Amanda Boulter

A Faerhaven Press Book
www.faerhavenpress.com

Find more Little Moose books,
stories and free gifts at

www.littlemooseandwolfie.com

Concept and text by Leo & Amanda
Illustration by Leo

Design in Serif PagePlus by Leo & Amanda
Font, Little Moose, created by Leo

A LITTLE MOOSE and WOLFIE Book

A DOG'S GUIDE to DRAGONS

Leo Hartas
&
Amanda Boulter

FAERHAVEN PRESS

For
Dylan and Robyn
Who both love dragons

With special thanks to
Inky and Dracula
(the cats)
who know nothing about dragons

"Always remember, it's simply not
an adventure worth telling
if there aren't any dragons."
Sarah Ban Breathnach

Dragons are everywhere.

Most humans don't believe that,
But it's true.

Wolfie knows all
about dragons.

Little Moose knows
all about them too,
but not as much as
Wolfie.

Even the best
humans don't always
see what's in front
of them.

Wolfie says there are five kinds of dragons.

Tree dragons are the littlest.
Water dragons are the middlest.
And rock dragons are the biggest.

Fire dragons come in every size
and are always swooping about.
That's why even humans can see
fire dragons.

Spirit dragons come in all sizes
too. They can be as big as
a mountain or as small
as a bird.

But humans can only
glimpse spirit dragons
from the corner
of their eye.

In the eye of the storm,
there be dragons

Big kiss

Dragons are closely related to birds

Dragons do not make good house pets

Oh no! A terrifying dragon!

Dragons are rainy day friends

Dragons love to snuggle

Babysitting the kids next door

Never listen to advice
from a dragon pup

Dragons can be so embarrassing

Dragons are great for nosegrinds, tailslides and wingflips

Never feed a dragon baked beans

Flying first class

Hedge dragons love surprises

To make a dragon go faster
just pull on his ears

With rock dragons
it's a whole different ball game

Never ask a dragon to light your fire

Hop on!

That was so cool!

Dogs don't believe in dragon runes

Dragons love having their teeth cleaned

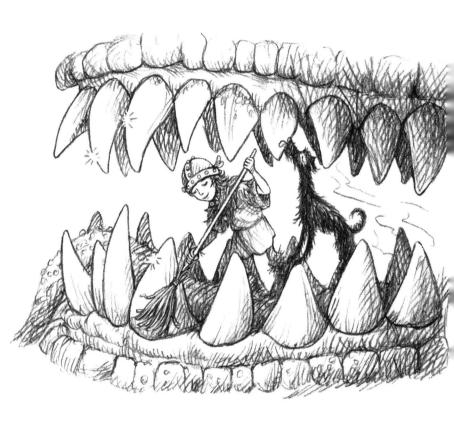

Make sure you get
right to the back

Moosing around

Rock dragons can get
a bit hot headed

This is not a dragon

...or this

Dragons love school trips

Everyone listens to the Dragon King

Dressed for battle

Don't worry Wolfie, he won't miss it!

Humans are more like dragons
than they think

Never go into a smoking cave

Varoom!
Go Team Dragon!

Tree dragons are very picky eaters

Dogs hate hot baths!

Always take your shoes off before
bouncing on a dragon

Dragons love sharing a campfire

And sleepovers are best of all

Even more moosing around

Duck!
Low flying dragons!

Fishing dragons are just weird

Hear the water dragons roar

Are you sure this is a cave?

Dragons are easy to sniff out

Surfing a dragon wave

Just hanging

Whoosh!

Don't blink or you'll miss it!

Ssh! Keep still

Swimming lessons

Spirit dragons are always
watching over us

And they'll always be there
when we need them

A glimpse into
the world of
Little Moose
and Wolfie

Through the Dragon's Throat
Across the Darkwater
Beneath the Wall
At the Edge of the World
Lies the village of Faerhaven

And there
Under the watchful eye of Odin
Lives a boy called Little Moose
(and Wolfie)

Faerhaven

FAERHAVEN

Over the Darkwater

DARKWATER

~The Dragon's Throat

FYLKEFJORD

Follow the adventures of Little Moose
from a baby to a young adult

Look out for these new series coming soon

A LITTLE MOOSE and WOLFIE Book

LITTLE MOOSE
loves his
NEW PUPPY

Leo
Hartas

Amanda
Boulter

FAERHAVEN PRESS

Playful tales for toddlers

Exciting picture
books and chapter
books for early
and confident
readers

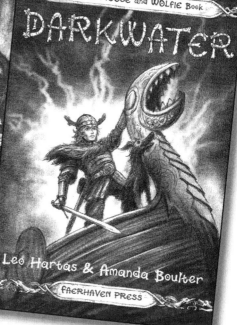

Challenging
adventures for
teens and young adults

Out now
on Amazon

A LITTLE MOOSE and WOLFIE Book

MINDFULNESS for VIKINGS

Leo Hartas & Amanda Boulter

FAERHAVEN PRESS

MINDFULNESS for VIKINGS

Despite their fearsome reputation for blood curdling battles and outrageous axe wielding, every Viking seeks inner calm.

Join Little Moose and his dog, Wolfie, as they find gentle happiness through adventure, play and just moosing around.

A book of inspirational sayings and delightful illustrations that helps adults and children appreciate the simple pleasures in life.

I am the storm!

Finding balance

SEA DRAGON

FREE PLAY SET

Sign up to our mailing list to get this
fabulous free gift
to download, print and make.

www.littlemooseandwolfie.com

Leo Hartas has been illustrating children's books, magazines, comics and games for over 30 years. He loves running around the fields of Devon, England, dressed as Viking and hunting for dragons. He lives in a tumbledown cottage with two cats, one with a little black nose called Inky and a big white fluffy one called Dracula.

Amanda Boulter has spent many hours contemplating the dragons in her own life and finding the courage to look them in the eye. She teaches creative writing at the University of Winchester, England.

Wolfie would love to hear from you
wolfie@littlemooseandwolfie.com

And if you love dragons like Wolfie
does, please leave us a review

Made in the USA
Middletown, DE
11 July 2018